4/6

6

Tiger D~~~~
Tiger Dead!

Stories from the Caribbean

Contents

Illustrated by Satoshi Kitamura

⟡ Collins

Tiger Dead! Tiger Dead!

by Grace Nichols

Chapter 1

One day Tiger was strolling through the forest and stopping every few moments to admire his stripy face in a stream. Times were hard and suddenly an idea came to Tiger's head that it would be nice to have the forest all to himself. To himself and his family of course.

The more Tiger thought about it, the more he fell in love with the idea, until he began to speak his feelings aloud: "Imagine me roving freely. Me and my family will have all this to ourselves. No Monkey, Snake, Turtle and the rest to pester me. I must think of a plan to get rid of them, especially that troublesome spider-person who calls himself Anansi. I will play dead to catch the living."

3

Tiger was so taken up with himself that he didn't see Anansi himself sitting on top of a palm tree. Anansi, that tricky little spider-man, was the last person Tiger would have wanted to overhear him.

And guess what? Anansi had listened to every single word.

Well, as soon as Tiger got home he told his wife about the plan he had to become king of the jungle.

4

The plan was simple. He, Tiger, would pretend to be dead and all the animals would be invited to his home. His wife would allow them, one by one, to go into a back room and see the body. As each animal passed by, he, Tiger, would rise up and hit each one down with a big stick. Tiger's children would then drag the bodies away.

Tiger and his wife held on to each other's stripes and laughed until eye-water came to their eyes. What a plan!

Well, bright and early next morning, Mrs Tiger set out
blowing a big conch shell through the forest.
When everyone had gathered, she burst into tears,
telling them about the sudden death of her husband
and inviting them to the funeral. As expected,
the news was a big shock.

"Tiger dead! Tiger dead!" was the cry everywhere.
The news shook the forest. For the rest of the day no
one could do anything but talk of the death of Tiger.

"It beats me," said Brother Snake, "it really beats me. Only yesterday I saw Tiger walking along looking strong-strong."

"Must be a heart attack or something," said Sister Turtle. "Here today, gone tomorrow, eh?"

Only Anansi wasn't present.

Chapter 2

The next day, all the animals gathered at the home of Tiger for the funeral. They had something to eat as was the custom, and stood around waiting for Mrs Tiger to tell them when to go in and see the body. Tiger, meanwhile, was lying inside, muffling his laughter with a pillow.

Anansi was the last to arrive. He came in style, in his best funeral suit, hat and bow tie. After taking one look at the other crying animals, he drew Mrs Tiger aside and began to talk in a loud voice. Loud enough for both the weeping animals and Tiger inside to hear him.

"Madam," he began, "no one is sorrier than me about Brother Tiger. When I got the news, I myself had to lie down in bed. But are you sure-sure that he's dead?"

"Sure, Anansi!" cried Mrs Tiger. "Who would know better than me who held his hand as he gave his last gasp?" She didn't like Anansi being so nosy.

"Poor Tiger, he was my best friend, you know, Mrs Tiger," went on Anansi, lying through his teeth. "Can I be the first one to go in and see him?"

"I see no reason why not, Anansi," said Mrs Tiger shortly. It would serve him right to be the first one to get the chop, she thought.

Anansi made sure he had a bite to eat and a drink before chatting with the other animals for a while.

Soon it was time to go in and see Tiger's body. Tiger grinned, clutching his stick as he waited. He knew that Anansi would be the first one coming. But as he waited, he suddenly heard Anansi saying loudly, "Oh, I completely forgot to ask, Mrs Tiger. Has Tiger sneezed?"

"Sneezed, Anansi?" asked Mrs Tiger in amazement.
"You've come to make fun of a poor widow.
Whoever heard of the dead sneezing?"

"Ah, madam," said Anansi, "you have no experience.
I have in my travels seen many a tiger die and believe
me, no tiger is truly dead until he has sneezed three
times. Every good doctor will tell you that.
Take comfort, Mrs Tiger. Since your husband hasn't
sneezed, he isn't really dead. He will get better."

Mrs Tiger and the other animals listened to Anansi with open mouths. Nobody had heard that one before. Tiger lying under his sheet could not believe his ears, either. If what Anansi said was true, then the animals would think that he wasn't really dead and that would spoil all his plans.

So there and then, Tiger thought to himself, "I'd better sneeze, now."

"Aaahtishoo! Aaahtishoo! Aaahtishoo!"

Tiger gave three loud sneezes.

And that was all it took to send the animals hurrying back to their homes and Anansi laughing, *"Kee-Kee-Kee!"* to the top of his tree.

"Tiger got muscles, but Anansi got brains," was his only comment.

14

Owl and Belle-Belle

by John Agard

Chapter 1

There was Owl thinking to himself, "I wish, I wish,
I was as handsome as my cousin Rooster. Eyes turn
when Rooster enters a room. Everybody says, 'What
a good-looking fellow!' But me, who would fancy me,
with my puffed-out cheeks and popping-out eyes?
I guess I'll never get married. No, no wedding bells
will ring for Owl."

But one evening Owl met a girl who smiled at him.
Owl felt sure that if she had seen his face by
daylight, she wouldn't be smiling at him. Yet this girl
was smiling at him now. Not only that, she started
talking to him.

"Don't you love the darkness?" she said to Owl.
"I could sit forever on the veranda and watch night
fall over the mountain top. It's so peaceful to
daydream in the dark."

Owl agreed and thought she spoke very nicely.
And he liked her even more for saying that she liked
the dark. Why couldn't he visit her in the evening?
That way, she wouldn't have to see his face
by daylight.

So when Belle-Belle – for that was the girl's name –
invited him to her house, Owl just couldn't wait.
He counted the hours, the minutes, the seconds.

And on the stroke of seven he visited her the next
night. And he visited her the next night and the next
night and the next night, always wearing a straw hat
to hide his face. They would sit on the veranda
talking politely and betting each other who would be
first to spot a firefly or a falling star.

18

But he always made sure that he
arrived at seven, sharp.
And the moment her grandmother
began coughing and shifting in
her rocking chair, Owl knew it was
9 o'clock and time to leave.

Now, the grandmother didn't mind
Owl visiting her granddaughter.
But why did he always choose
evening to visit? And why that wide
straw hat, always over his face?

Belle-Belle explained that Owl
worked hard all day and needed
to go home and freshen up.
Besides she felt the straw hat
suited him.

19

But her grandmother had long made up her mind to get a good look at his face. "Better to see his face by day, just in case these visits lead to marriage-talk. Let's invite him to a dance this coming Sunday afternoon. I'm sure he won't be working."

So that was agreed.

What was Owl to do? He couldn't refuse the invitation. He hadn't been to a dance for a while and looked forward to shaking a leg. But why did it have to be afternoon?

Chapter 2

Owl had to find a way out. So on Sunday, he asked his cousin Rooster, already in his party clothes, to explain that he'd be late. "Make some excuse for me. Say something urgent cropped up. Say my roof was leaking. I hate lying but I can't bear for this girl to see my face in full daylight."

So Rooster, with his little red necktie, strutted to the dance and announced to all that Owl was running late. "Owl sends his apologies," he said. "But he'll soon come."

On the stroke of seven, no need to guess who arrived. Owl, of course, who else? And by that time the dance was in full swing. Owl could see his cousin Rooster dancing in a circle with all the girls.

He made a sign for Rooster to come over. "Do me
a favour, Cous," Owl whispered. "Keep a look-out for
the first sign of daylight and give me a shout.
As soon as you crow your *Ko-kee-o-ko Ko-kee-o-ko*,
I'll know it's time to leave."

When the girl's grandmother offered to take his hat,
Owl made some excuse about a wire fence scratching
his face, and he was glad when Belle-Belle came over
and asked him to dance.

23

So they went outside into the yard where the band was playing. The fiddle sounded so sweet, Owl found himself humming close to Belle-Belle's cheek as they danced. She thought he was a lovely dancer and there was kindness in his voice, even if he had a strange way of wearing his hat.

Once or twice, Owl begged to be excused and went to keep an eye on the horizon for himself, just in case Rooster forgot to warn him that daylight was near. He knew what his cousin was like. Already, Rooster looked like he was in his own world, dancing with Belle-Belle's best friend.

But just as darkness can come sudden-sudden to
the mountain top, daylight can spring just as sudden.
Soon, sunrise was catching them. And when Rooster
sounded his *Ko-kee-o-ko Ko-kee-o-ko*, it was too late.
The yard was already catching the first rays of sunlight.

Before Owl could leave, the grandmother had pulled
the straw hat from his face. "About time we saw
your face! No reason for a polite young man like you
to keep on hat inside house! You have something
to hide?"

Owl didn't waste time replying. He rushed out the door trying to cover his face. But not before Belle-Belle had caught a glimpse of him. She liked his chubby cheeks and sensitive eyes that popped out like two little moon-spectacles. She thought it was the most handsome face she'd ever seen.

"Wait, Owl, wait!" she called out. But Owl had gone. He didn't even turn back for his hat.

Owl left the party feeling sad. Belle-Belle didn't fancy him after all. And who could blame her? Maybe she'd seen his face and those puffed-out eyes. Maybe it was Rooster who made her heart flutter.

Rooster meanwhile was still sounding his *Ko-kee-o-ko Ko-kee-o-ko*, even after his cousin had gone. And by then he was so merry, he even proposed marriage to Belle-Belle's best friend.

As Rooster was leaving the party, Belle-Belle drew him aside and whispered, "Rooster, you must tell your cousin Owl for me that he has a very handsome face. Tell him come visit me tomorrow. Day or night, any time that suits him. I will be keeping his hat safe for him."

Rooster couldn't wait to get home and tell Owl what Belle-Belle had whispered with her dreamy smile.

The news brought blushes to Owl's face and Rooster was so pleased for his cousin. "Lucky you, lucky you!" said Rooster. "That girl Belle-Belle has a sweet-eye for you!"

To cut a long story short, Rooster was best man at the wedding of Owl and Belle-Belle, who made a lovely couple.

Owl got himself a new straw hat for the big day, but Belle-Belle always kept the old one to remind her of their first falling-in-love days.

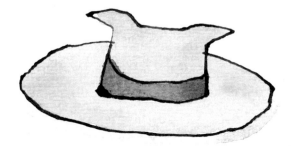

29

Owl's Feelings Roller Coaster

2 Hope: Owl meets Belle-Belle and she invites him home.

4 Relief: Owl decides to visit when it's dark, wearing a hat to hide his face.

1 Gloom: Owl thinks no one will fancy him because he's not handsome.

3 Fear: Owl worries that Belle-Belle will think he's ugly.

5 Fear: Belle-Belle and her granny invite Owl to a dance in daylight.

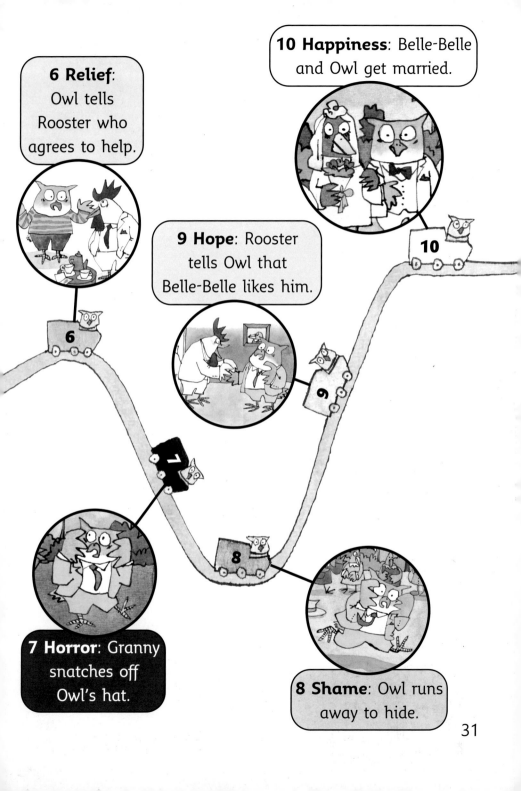

6 Relief: Owl tells Rooster who agrees to help.

10 Happiness: Belle-Belle and Owl get married.

9 Hope: Rooster tells Owl that Belle-Belle likes him.

7 Horror: Granny snatches off Owl's hat.

8 Shame: Owl runs away to hide.

31

❣️ Ideas for guided reading ❣️

Learning objectives: identify and make notes of the main points of the main sections of text; infer characters' feelings in fiction; empathise with characters and debate moral dilemmas portrayed in texts; use some drama strategies to explore stories or issues

Curriculum links: Geography: Passport to the world; Citizenship:

Living in a diverse world; ICT: Combining Text and Graphics

Interest words: Caribbean, roving, troublesome, Anansi, conch shell, veranda, marriage-talk, sensitive, moon-spectacles, roller coaster

Resources: ICT, whiteboards, outline of a tiger and an owl, story skeleton

Getting started

This book can be read over two or more guided reading sessions.

- Ask children to recall any animal stories that they know and the key characteristics of the animals featured (this could be from a book or film text, e.g. *Peter Rabbit*; the mouse in *The Gruffalo*; *The Lion King*, *The Jungle Book*).

- Look at the front and back covers. Identify the creatures shown (tiger, spider, owl). Discuss what characteristics they might have.

- Read the blurb to the children. List some words that can be used to describe Tiger and Owl, e.g. *Tiger: mean, selfish, greedy; Owl: timid, nervous, anxious.*

Reading and responding

- Read pp2–3 to the children. Discuss what may be meant by Tiger's words *"I will play dead to catch the living."* Check that children understand why Tiger wants the forest to himself. Add more words to describe Tiger's character and feelings to the list.

- Explain that Anansi the spider is a famous trickster in Caribbean stories who often tries to trick other animals.